Felix,
Puss in Boots

by Maeve Friel

Illustrated by Beccy Blake

FRANKLIN WATTS
LONDON•SYDNEY

First published in 2013 by
Franklin Watts
338 Euston Road
London
NW1 3BH

Franklin Watts Australia
Level 17/207 Kent Street
Sydney
NSW 2000

Text © Maeve Friel 2013
Illustration © Beccy Blake 2013

A CIP catalogue record for this book is available
from the British Library.

ISBN 978 1 4451 1615 0 (hbk)
ISBN 978 1 4451 1621 1 (pbk)

Series Editor: Jackie Hamley
Series Advisor: Catherine Glavina
Series Designer: Peter Scoulding

Printed in China

Franklin Watts is a divison of
Hachette Children's Books,
an Hachette UK company.
www.hachette.co.uk

Felix looked at the cat
on the TV.

"I want to be like that cat,"
Felix thought. "I want to be
Puss in Boots."

Felix smiled at Princess, the cat from next door.

Princess washed her face.

Felix turned cartwheels round and round the garden.

One, two, three, four!

9

He danced along the fence.
"Take that, Buster!"

He made a flying leap
onto the apple tree.

Oh no! Ouch!

Felix saw stars.
He crashed into the
washing pole.

Down came all the clothes.

Felix was trapped!

"Help!" miaowed Felix.

Everyone came running.

Poor Felix.

He was bleeding.

His paws were cut.

His eye looked bad.

Mum called the vet.

20

Felix had to lie on the table. Felix had to say "Aaaah!"

The vet took his
temperature. She looked
at his cut paws. She gave
him a jab.

Felix needed stitches in both his back paws.
He had to have stitches in his face.

He was very brave.

"What a soldier," said Dad.

Back at home, Felix saw himself.

"I can't wear a lampshade.
I can't wear boots,"
he miaowed.

"Some cats can wear boots," purred Princess. "Puss in Boots can."

Felix gave her a big smile.

Puzzle 1

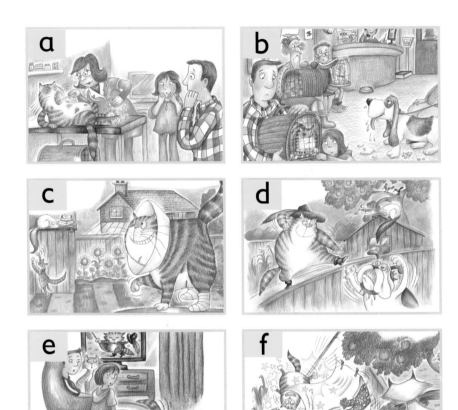

Put these pictures in the correct order.
Now tell the story in your own words.
How short can you make the story?

Puzzle 2

excited   confused

tired

worried   cross

glad

Choose the word which best describes each character. Can you think of any more? Pretend to be one of the characters!

Answers

Puzzle 1

The correct order is:

1e, 2d, 3f, 4b, 5a, 6c

Puzzle 2

Felix The correct word is excited.

The incorrect words are confused, tired.

Dad The correct word is worried.

The incorrect words are cross, glad.

Look out for more Leapfrog stories:

For details of all our titles go to: www.franklinwatts.co.uk

*hardback